CRESCENT CITY C...
COMPREHENSI...

TABLE OF CONTENTS

INTRODUCTION..2

ABOUT HOODOO..3

COMMON HOODOO TERMS...4

CANDLES...5

GRIS GRIS..8

SPIRITUAL BATHS...11

CONJURE OILS..13

CONJURE POWDERS...20

SPIRITUAL SOAPS...23

CURIOS..25

INK...28

INCENSE..29

CLOSING WORDS..30

INTRODUCTION

Crescent City Conjure proudly presents this comprehensive guide to working with all of the spiritual tools that we offer. We pride ourselves on our authenticity and the detail that goes into crafting each of our products, and we want to ensure that you have the instructions you need to apply them correctly. Each tool has been blessed by a skilled conjure man to imbue them with the power to create the changes that you desire.

We've included necessary direction and little tips that could be helpful in your work. Our product selection is always growing. If you don't see a particular product listed, it is likely that it was created after the publication of the booklet. We will be updating the product list in this booklet once a year. You can find further details about each product at **www.crescentcityconjure.us.**

While we've done our best to share essential information, each specific situation is unique and may require methods that are not listed in order to see success in your work. If you are still unsure about how to use any of our products please contact us at **crescentcityconjure@gmail.com** or come see us in person at our shop in New Orleans.

In the tradition of hoodoo, faith is the anchor that empowers our work. It is important to be confident and strong willed in your ability to manifest your desired change before beginning the work. We wish you much luck in your magical endeavors.

__Blessings from Sen Elias and all of us at Crescent City Conjure!__

About Hoodoo
African American Folk Magic

Hoodoo (also known as rootwork or conjure) is an African American folk magic that has strong roots here in the South. The history of hoodoo practice and how it began is a powerful story of survival against incredible odds. The story begins in the 1500s when the the triangular trade route of the transatlantic slave trade was used to transport more than 10 million enslaved Africans across the Atlantic Ocean to the Americas.

The men and women who survived the journey lost everything. The only thing that couldn't be taken from them was their spiritual beliefs. The spiritual practices of the slave community evolved in the New World due to necessity and through the communal sharing of knowledge among themselves, Native Americans, and Europeans settlers. The results of their combined knowledge
and wisdom were passed on orally from generation to generation and became known as the tradition of hoodoo.

"The Devil's shoestring looks just like a fern with a lot of roots.
My mother used to grow them in the corner of our garden. They are lucky."

—as related by Mrs. Avery from "Slave Narratives: A Folk History of Slavery
in the United States from Interviews with Former Slaves"
by the Work Projects Administration.

Our ancestors knew that there is power in all of God's creation. The Earth and all living things that inhabit the Earth have a spirit. Every plant and animal has a signature. Our ancestors knew how to tap into the power that resides in the signatures of herbs and roots. Rootwork is the ability to elevate, combine, and secure the spirits of natural elements in such a way that they work together towards a unified goal.

GLOSSARY
COMMON HOODOO TERMS

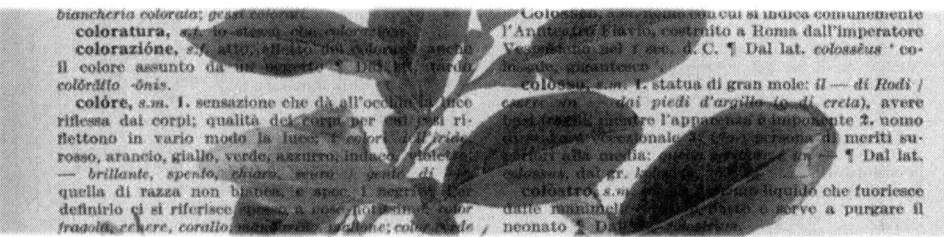

These instructions are a basic guideline for working with your new spiritual tools. The more energy and focus you give to working with these tools, the more likely it is that you'll see results. In this reading, you may encounter unfamiliar words and phrases. Please read through the following terms, as they are commonly used in hoodoo practice.

"Fixed" - Something that is "fixed" has undergone a process of blessing that includes the use of oils and herbs. Fixing an object imbues it with the spiritual power that is used to manifest our prayers. Candles are often fixed to be used in rituals.

"Dressed" - The necessary oils, herbs, or other ingredients that have been added to our spiritual tool. When something has been dressed, it indicates that the tool is fixed (see "fixed" meaning) and ready to be worked.

"Feeding" – We must maintain the spiritual power of a charm by adding outside ingredients. Oils, alcohols, tobacco, or incense smoke are often used to "feed" charms. Feeding is done at scheduled times and for the duration of the use of the charm.

"Target" - The specific person or place we hope to affect in our workings.

"Personal Concerns" - The specific belongings of a person, place, or thing. Personal concerns include anything that contains the DNA of a target or material that has closely interacted with our target (like clothing). Hair, nails, blood, and other bodily fluids are all considered personal concerns. The picture, name, and date of birth of a person can also be used to establish a connection.

"Petition Paper" – Traditionally, petitions are written on small squares of brown paper bags. Write prayers, spells, and invocations on the pieces of paper to add details to workings. Prayers, commands, and specifics concerning a desired outcome can be written on a petition papers. We fold petitions three times (directed away from ourselves) if we hope to send a person or situation away from us. Likewise, we fold three times towards ourselves to attract people or blessings.

"Wax Reading" – A search for significant signs and symbols within dried melted wax. These shades and symbols can give us insight into how our work many manifest.

Candles

Seven-Day Fixed Candles

Our fixed seven-day candles arrive to our clients completely dressed.

- Remove the plastic top.
- On the top of the candle add a small amount of your personal concerns or your targets personal concerns (hair, blood or nails). Adding the personal concerns instructs the candle on who should receive the prayers that you will say in your work.
- Place your petition paper under your candle.
- On the first night, after lighting your candle, spend 10 to 15 minutes focused on your desired outcome in front of your candle while it burns. During that time, you can say appropriate prayers or invocations.
- Every night that your candles burns you should spend 5 to 10 minutes in meditation with your candle.
- When the work is done, dispose of the candle and petition in a place that seems appropriate to the work (ie. church, bank, river, cemetery, etc.).

NOTE: The candle should stay lit from first time you light it until it completely burning out. You may place the candle in a bowl of water if you are concerned with fire safety.

We Offer:

"Do As I Say" Seven-Day Candle
"Blockbusting" Seven-Day Candle
"Open Roads" Seven-Day Candle
"Money Drawing" Seven-Day Candle
"Dume" Seven-Day Candle

FIGURE CANDLES

Figure candles do not arrive dressed.
For best results use an appropriate oil and powder to fix these candles for workings.

- Carve either your name and date of birth into the candle or your intended target's name and date of birth.
- Create a petition paper and place it underneath the figure candle. For the entire time that the candle is burning focus on your intended goal.
- After the candle burns all the way down you may choose to read the wax if you like. Dispose of the candle and petition at an appropriate location (ie. church, bank, river, cemetery, etc.).

NOTE: Figure candles are known to burn very quickly, so utilize every minute to work. You can split the work up over days by extinguishing the flame of the candle before it's done burning.

WE OFFER:

Lover's Embrace
Black Male • White Male
Black Female • White Female
Black Skull • Red Skull
White Skull

Hand-Poured Candles

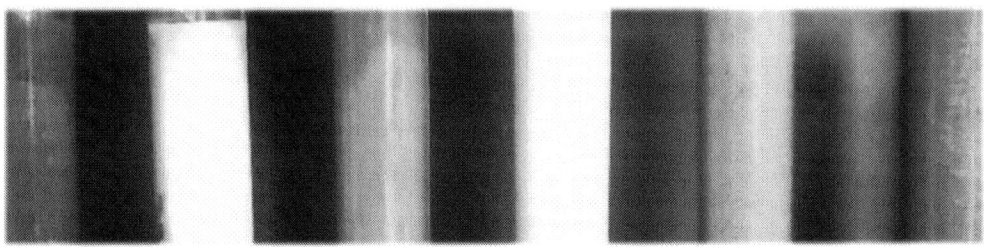

Our hand-poured candles come completely dressed and fixed.

The wax on these candles melts quickly so they can be worked over the space of a night, or split up to work over several nights by extinguishing the flame before it burns all the way down.

- Carve either your name and date of birth into the candle or your intended target's name and date of birth.
- Create a petition paper and place it underneath the figure candle. For the entire time that the candle is burning, focus on your intended goal.
- After the candle burns all the way down you may choose to read the wax if you like. When the work is done, dispose of the candle and petition at an appropriate location (ie. church, bank, river, cemetery, etc.).

We Offer:

Uncrossing
Happy Home
Fiery Protection
Love's True Kiss
Ancestor Awakening
Fast Luck
Banishing

A Guide to Using Gris Gris

What is a gris gris?

The simple answer: often called a "hand" (as in helping hand), a gris gris is a little spirit companion that has the ability to assist in a desired goal.

Each ingredient in the bag is carefully selected by the conjure man to work in unison to bring about a desired change.

Our organs work to power our body. A gris gris' organs are its roots, minerals, bones, and stones. This is where the gris gris' power comes from. For this reason, gris gris' have their own type of consciousness. They must be "fed" (see glossary of terms) like any other living entity to continue to work. Traditionally, the hand is fed liquor, tobacco, and even blood to impart some of the energy that resides in those substances.

The more a gris gris is handled, the more we impart our energy to it. It's important to know that gris gris bags are limited in their power. The unified spirit of these bags are the coming together of roots, which have simple spirits. We wouldn't expect to win the lottery with a money drawing hand, but we would expect to get that promotion we've been wanting. It's important to know and understand how this type of magic works in order to utilize it for its highest benefit.

In the following we pages we will learn how to use the various gris gris' that Crescent City Conjure offers our clients...

CROWN OF SUCCESS
For the ambitious go-getter.

This gris gris is best used by people who own businesses or depend on client relationships to actuate income. Success is not necessarily only about money; it's also about the bigger picture of achieving larger goals. This gris gris' job is to create favorable connections that lead to opportunities for us to achieve personal success. This gris gris works to put you in the right place at the right time. Keep the gris gris in your right pocket to project success in meetings. Carry it in your left pocket to attract success when opportunities present themselves. Feed the gris gris rum and Crescent City Conjure's own Crown of Success Oil once a week.

MONEY DRAWING
For the financially motivated.

When an increase in finances is needed use this gris gris; especially when money is short, to ease financial stresses, or when on the hunt for a new job. This gris gris often results in surprise income or finally receiving money that is owed to you. Carry it to job interviews in your left pocket. Feed the gris gris rum and Crescent City Conjure's own Money Drawing Oil once a week.

FIERY PROTECTION
For the survivor.

The best form of protection is preparedness and a constant awareness of our surroundings. Physical protections are important, but no matter how secure we feel we are, there are always blind spots and unpredictable dangers. This gris gris can be used as a mirror that enables us to see into these blind spots. Place this gris gris in the car, above doors, on the desk at work, or anywhere added protection is needed. The best way to use it is to carry it with you anywhere and everywhere. Feed this gris gris with rum and Crescent City Conjure's own Fiery Protection Oil once a week.

LOVE DRAWING GRIS GRIS
For all the lovers.

To attract a lover, carry this gris gris everyday. This is not to make a specific person fall in love with you, but to attract the right person for you specifically, at the right time. Carry it in your left pocket for attraction. Speak the traits you hope to see in your love, but try not to be too specific. Instead, ask for qualities like loyalty, humor, stability, etc. Best used in social environments where the opportunity to meet someone is most likely (ie. the bar, a party or gathering, school). Feed this gris gris rum and Crescent City Conjure's own Love Drawing Oil once a week.

SPIRIT CALLING GRIS GRIS
For the spiritual seeker.

Use this gris gris to increase spiritual awareness. Place the gris gris under your pillow at nighttime to cause lucid, prophetic, or especially vivid dreams. Place on your ancestor altar to better hear the words of the spirits you work with. Carry it with you to stay open to "hearing" and seeing the insight of your guiding spirits. Feed this gris gris rum and either Crescent City Conjure's own Ancestor Oil or Witch Doctor Oil once a week.

HEXING GRIS GRIS
For our enemies.

The Hexing Gris Gris is not meant to be worn. It was created to negatively affect our enemies by placing it somewhere they are sure walk over. Bury this gris gris in the yard of bad neighbors or under the desk of troublesome co-workers. You may place this hand anywhere you want negative energy to effect a target. Take extra care to make sure that it won't be found, and also to ensure your own protection while using it.

SPIRITUAL BATHS

WHAT ARE SPIRITUAL BATHS AND HOW ARE THEY USED?

At Crescent City Conjure, all of our spiritual baths are crafted from a recipe of herbs and roots that are carefully chosen to heal spiritual damage and support spiritual growth. The healing effects of these baths are known to relieve stress, lessen emotional trauma, break curses, and cut negative ties. The spirits of the herbs and roots work together to pull off the negative weight that aggravates feelings of depression or a lack of motivation. Many of Crescent City Conjure's clients report experiencing an emotional release during their baths—a release that provides the therapy of confronting old attachments while enabling us to move forward with a fresh perspective.

Spiritual baths are a staple in any conjure worker's routine because they are a simple and easy way to maintain spiritual hygiene while also breaking any spells that may have been laid against the worker. The baths can be used in the shower, so don't worry if your living quarters don't include a tub.

IN A SHOWER: the bath is applied by using a cup or pan to pour a small amount of liquid over large areas of your body (the top of the head, chest, shoulders, back, legs, feet) and then using your hands to wipe the bath ingredients off in a downward motion starting from the top of your head and ending at your feet. This downward motion enforces the baths intention to clear undesired attachments, it also allows you to completely cover any areas that may have been missed.

IN A BATH TUB: begin by filling the tub with water. After the tub is full, say a prayer over the water to rid it of any negative energy it may carry. We suggest using Psalms 31; if you do not prefer to use the Bible in your workings, any prayer said honestly and from the heart will work. Pour half of the bath mixture into the water and soak for 15-minutes. Remember to stay focused on the release of any negative attachments you hold onto.

After applying the bath mixture in the shower or in a bath, do not use a towel to dry off, air dry instead. You want the mixture to remain on the skin, where it will continue to work. Do not use soap with the baths, as you don't want the ingredients of the soap to compete with the herbs in the bath recipe. After you are dry, do your best to stay in solitude. This can most easily be achieved by taking the bath right before going to sleep. Depending on the severity of your trauma, you should repeat the bath for a regimen of either three, seven, or nine nights in a row.

After using a spiritual bath, you should immediately experience a renewed sense of peace and clarity. If you're using the baths over the space of days, common results may include:

- The shedding of detrimental habits.
- The clearing of depression and/or anxieties.
- Increased awareness of negative people and places.
- Increased motivation to make positive changes in your life.
- Increased daily energy.
- Various things in daily life working in your favor.
- An overall more positive disposition.

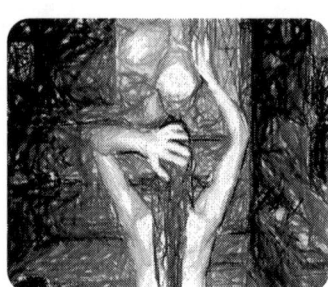

Perhaps most importantly, any hexes or curses that may have been laid on you should be broken after only three days of a spiritual bath.

WE OFFER:

Fire Bath
Get Yo Mind Right Bath
Devil Be Gone Bath
Heed My Command Bath

CONJURE OILS

WHAT ARE CONJURE OILS AND HOW ARE THEY USED?

The oils that are used in hoodoo, rootwork, and conjure, are fascinating because they are the most versatile carrier for a hoodoo recipe. In the oils, we blend herbs, roots, and other materials to cause a spiritual change to occur. Conjure oils can be applied in many different ways. They can be used to dress oneself, to dress articles of clothing, and in our more malevolent works they can be used against our enemies by dressing their car handles, items at their place of work, or anywhere they are known to visit on a regular basis.

Some of our oils are traditional hoodoo recipes and others are created by the conjure man using his experience and expertise to craft new and effective blends. Our clients' numerous testimonials have proven time and time again that our oils at Crescent City Conjure bring strong results.

In the following pages we will discuss the various methods of applying our oils, both generally speaking as well as specifically to each oil...

How to Use Conjure Oils
Dressing Candles and Gris Gris

One of the most common ways to apply a conjure oil is to **anoint candles** with them, and any of our oils can be used to bless candles.. A candle that is anointed with a conjure oil becomes a carrier for the recipe. The candle can then be used in a specific way to bring about the changes you seek.

Oils are also necessary to feed **gris gris.** A few drops of the appropriate oil are applied to the ball of the gris gris so that the spirit will continue to work for you.

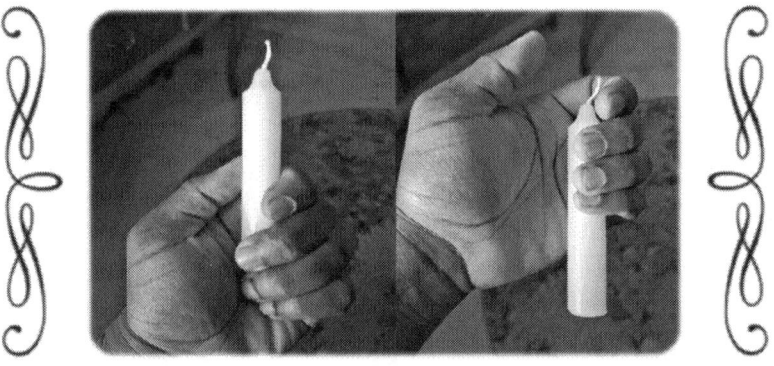

To dress a plain candle with our conjure oil, pour a small amount of the oil onto the palm of your hand. If your goal to attract something to you, use your hand to evenly distribute the *oils from the top of the candle to the bottom*. If you are trying to banish or send something away from you, *use the same motion from the bottom to the top of the candle*. You can use this method with our figure candles, taper candles, and pillar candles. For seven-day candles pour a small amount of oil onto the top of the candle. Be wary of using excess oil when dressing a seven-day candle, as you can accidentally drown the wick.

IMPORTANT NOTE: Please exhibit caution when using potentially dangerous oils for negative workings (such as our Black Arts Oil or Banishing Oil) and *always* use gloves and newspaper to avoid any contact with your own skin and surrounding surfaces.

How to Use Conjure Oils

Wearing Oils

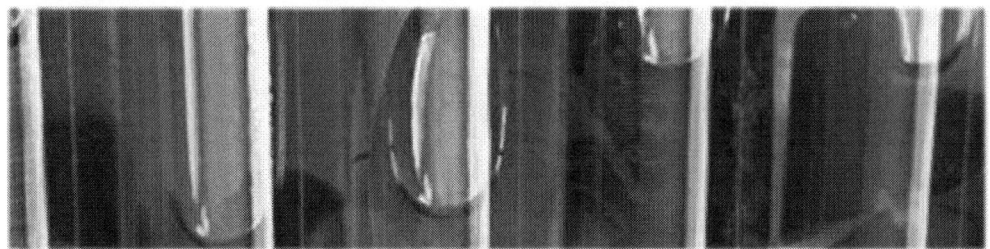

I keep several oils on my ancestor altar and every day during my morning devotions, I anoint myself with an oil that I think will support my goals for that day. It's important to note that not all of oils are to be worn. Some of the oils are intended to cause negative results and shouldn't come into contact with your skin. Please read through each description before using this method of self anointing. To attract something to you place a small amount of the appropriate oil on your left wrist if you are right handed and on your right wrist if you are left handed. Wipe the oil up your arm with the intention or receiving its qualities.

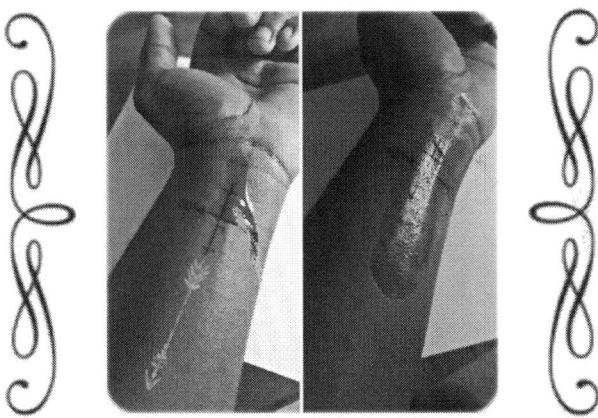

For oils that are intended to affect only you and not to attract something, place a small amount of oil on the back of your neck and the top of your head. You can also place a small amount of the appropriate oils on the bottom of your feet for protection or in the palms of your hands to influence others.

There are many ways to apply the oils and a particular situation may call for a more specific way to anoint yourself, so stay flexible and listen to your ancestors and intuition about where and how you should be applying the oils.

Conjure Oils

Our Products

For more detailed descriptions of our oils, visit us at www.crescentcityconjure.us.

Uncrossing

Use this oil to dress seven-day candles for uncrossing workings. You may also anoint yourself each day with the oil by applying a small amount to the back of your neck. If you happen to be bald, use this oil on the top of your head. After a spiritual bath, uncrossing oils may be used instead of moisturizing lotions.

Van Van

Best used on those "off" days that we all experience from time to time. Anoint yourself like you would a perfume or cologne. Also includes properties that have proven useful for repelling insects.

Crown of Success

Anoint your hands with this oil before business meetings. Place a small drop on the four corners of important documents or contracts that can lead to client acquisitions or winning favor in your professional environment. Dress your office door when working towards a promotion.

Fiery Protection

Use this oil almost anywhere that needs an added or extra layer of protection. Mark the front door of your home by drawing three X's on the door. Dress the bottom of your shoes to protect yourself from anyone who means to divert you from your path. Draw three X's on the wheels of your car or bike. As the wheels rotate, your protection will be enforced. Religious symbols may be dressed to enforce their protective powers.

High John the Conqueror

May be used as a component in all matters of money, legal cases, and domination. Anoint yourself with the oil when the immediate goal is to perhaps outsmart a competitor or find cunning ways to overcome difficult and tricky situations.

Happy Home

If somebody is causing problems in your home, find a way to apply the oil directly to the culprit. A small amount of oil can be used in the four corners of your home to uplift the energies there.

Lasting Love

Dress candles that are intended to cause love in your life. Wear this oil everyday to attract potential long term relationships. Also, feed your Lasting Love Gris Gris, add to oil lamps, and apply this oil to charms.

Fast Luck

Good for games of luck and turning one's luck from poor to fruitful. Dress two green dice with with our Fast Luck Oil and carry it in your left pocket with a piece of High John root or five finger root.

Money Drawing

Wear this oil while on the hunt for a new job to increase the chances of finding work. Dress bills and coins with this oil before depositing funds at the bank. Feed your Money Drawing Gris Gris with this oil and also rub a small amount into leather wallets or purses. Effectively used as a component in money drawing workings.

Follow Me Boy

Use this oil by anointing yourself before attending social functions where eligible men will be present. If you hope to gain the attention of a specific man, massage the oil onto him (with his consent) in an intimate way. Use this oil to dress male figure candles.

Follow Me Girl

Use this oil by anointing yourself before attending social functions where eligible women will be present. If you hope to gain the attention of a specific woman, massage the oil onto her (with her consent) in an intimate way. Use this oil to dress female figure candles.

BLOCKBUSTING

Dress blockbusting candles. Wear this oil when your goal is to break through the things that are blocking your path at work, at school, or in your personal life.

WITCH DOCTOR

Best used to enhance sensitivity to the spirits and energies that are called upon during spiritual workings. Our Witch Doctor Oil is intended to increase the ability to communicate and work with the invisible powers that are responsible for manifesting magical goals. Anoint yourself with this oil before any and all workings.

ANCESTOR OR GRAVEYARD

Dress your ancestor altar to increase communication with those in your family who have passed. Feed your Spirit Calling Gris Gris or anoint yourself with this oil before doing any work with the dead.

DOMINATION

Dress figure candles or seven day candles that have been fixed for your intended target. Use on petitions or charms intended to dominate a specific individual.

OPEN ROADS

Anoint yourself with our Open Roads Oil to increase opportunities and knock down the roadblocks that stand in the way of your progress. Use to dress road opening candles or charms.

SPIRIT OF NEW ORLEANS

Call on the unique spirit that can only be found in the magical city of New Orleans. Use this oil before magical workings by anointing yourself and your altars. Dress charms and candles that are intended to "shake up" the spirit of a place. Use this oil to better communicate with spirits that reside in New Orleans, such as Marie Laveau or Doctor John. Our Spirit of New Orleans Oil adds a little Creole spice to your spiritual work.

SWIFT CHANGE

Anoint yourself with this oil everyday while working to create change in your life. This oil works to create movement where you feel stagnant and we suggest that you wear it in the place you hope to see this movement. It's important that you know where you need change before wearing our Swift Change Oil. This oil is intended to be worn on a daily basis until the last drop is gone. By the time you finish the entire bottle you should see the changes you seek begin to take shape.

Win at Court

Begin to wear this oil for the three days leading up to any kind of court proceedings, on the day of court, and continue to anoint yourself with the oil for the three days following the court date. If used correctly, this oil can greatly increase the chances of winning any kind of legal case. You may also dress candles or charms for Win at Court workings.

Cut and Clear

This oil is intended to sever negative emotional attachments. Anoint yourself with our Cut and Clear Oil every time you have thoughts of or feelings for the person or situation you hope to distance yourself from. Apply a small amount to the center of your chest and the back of your neck. This oil should be used down to the last drop, so it's best to carry it on your persons throughout the day. You never know when old memories or emotions will present themselves! By the end of the bottle, any negative emotional attachments should be reversed. You may also use this oil in cut and clear workings by dressing candles and charms.

Separation & Banishing

Do not anoint yourself with this oil. Avoid skin contact by wearing gloves while handling. Use newspaper to avoid contact with surrounding surfaces, especially in your own home. This oil is intended to be used against anyone you wish to remove from your immediate environment. Get creative and find opportunities for your target to come into contact with the oil. You can place a small amount on door knobs, car handles, or items in their home or office. You may also dress figure candles with this oil.

Black Arts

Do not anoint yourself with this oil. This oil is intended to cause all manner of negativity. Avoid skin contact with this oil by wearing gloves while handling. Use newspaper to avoid contact with surrounding surfaces, especially in your own home. This oil is intended to be used against any person or situation you wish to curse. Get creative and find opportunities for your target to come into contact with the oil. Place a small amount on door knobs, car handles, or items in their home or office. You may also dress figure candles with this oil.

Conjure Powders

What are conjure powders and how are they used?

The powders that we use in hoodoo are unique blends of herbs, roots, and other natural materials, put together in such a way that they work towards one desired goal. The consistency of powders is the key to how they are used in workings. Unlike candles or charms, powders can be discreet enough to line doorways. The powder affects anyone who crosses the threshold and/or prevents enemies from entering across the threshold. Powders contain a number of highly effective ingredients but can be ground down to look like one ingredient, which prevents others from identifying its components.

Powders are versatile and may be applied to spiritual work in a variety of ways. Candles are usually dressed with powders and oils. In workings that contain liquids, it is better to use powders instead of oils because the powder will melt into the liquids (whereas oils do not blend as easily, if at all). Powders are very useful in magic that involves placing ingredients in a target's foot track (our Hot Foot Powder, for example). After carefully lining the insides of clothing with certain powders, we can take advantage of the ingredient's powers every time we wear that specific article of clothing.

For those who have never worked with hoodoo powders, we offer a selection of potent recipes that can be easily incorporated into a wide range of magical workings.

CONJURE POWDERS

OUR PRODUCTS

For more detailed descriptions of our powders, visit us online at www.crescentcityconjure.us.

HOT FOOT

Perhaps one of the most popular powder recipes, our Hot Foot Powder is made to compel our domestic enemies (neighbors, roommates, landlords, etc.) to move away from their place of residence. Use this powder by creating a thin line across the target's doorway or by placing a small amount of powder in their physical footprints. You may also use our Hot Foot Powder to dress candles in magical workings.

HAPPY HOME

Apply this powder in the four corners of your home to promote a calm and peaceful environment. Sprinkle a small amount under mattresses of housemates that cause drama and disagreements. Use to dress our Uncrossing Figure Candles or add our Happy Home Powder to a mojo bag.

MONEY DRAWING

This powder can be used in a variety of money drawing workings. Line the front door of your home or business to draw increased income. Add to lamp oils to "fix" the lamp for a money drawing working. Place a small amount of powder in your shoes before going out to hunt for a new job. Dress dollar bills before depositing them into the bank. You may also add our Money Drawing Powder to the inner lining of your personal work attire.

SILENCE THINE ENEMY POWDER

This is an old favorite in our personal powders inventory. Use to silence those who talk against your favor and those who slander your name. This powder is very effective in beef tongue or lime workings. Like our Hot Foot Powder, sprinkle a small amount in any spot that your target is sure to cross. You may also use this powder to dress our figure candles.

DOMINATION POWDER

Use this powder to bend others to your willpower to help to achieve whatever it is you desire from them. Our Domination Powder may be used to dress our seven day candles or figure candles. Add your own personal concerns to the powder and sprinkle some in rooms where business meetings will be held or places where you will be in competition with others.

PROTECTION POWDER

This powder can be used to line the front and back door of the home or anywhere you feel that added protection is needed (your primary vehicle, for example). You may also dress candles or add our Protection Powder to mojo bags.

ROAD OPENING POWDER

This powder can be used in all workings intended to increase the opportunities available to you. You may dress candles and charms, or use our Road Opening Powder in mojo bags and spiritual baths.

ANCESTOR POWDER

Use on ancestor altars to increase communication with those that have passed. You may also dress candles and create charms with our Ancestor Powder to be used in spirit communication.

Spiritual Soaps

WHAT ARE SPIRITUAL SOAPS AND HOW ARE THEY USED?

Spiritual soaps are made with a recipe of herbs and oils that have been blessed to support our specific goals through daily use. Every time we shower, we can take advantage of the spiritual benefits contained in these soaps. We wouldn't produce soap without considering how the base will affect the skin, so we've added oatmeal, shea butter and aloe to our blends. Soaps are a convenient way to support ongoing work and maintain our spiritual hygiene.

Our soaps are used much like our spiritual baths. Through contact with your skin, our herbal recipe can remove negative energy or assist us in working towards increased luck, love, and overall wellbeing. Soaps are no replacement for spiritual baths but they can extend the healing effects created by spiritual baths through daily use.

Creating our spiritual soaps requires a careful balance of soap base, oils, and herbs. In the end, we are left with an evenly distributed amount of each in every wash. Use Crescent City Conjure's spiritual soaps just like you would any bar of soap.

Spiritual Soaps
Our Products

For more detailed descriptions of our spiritual soaps, visit us online at www.crescentcityconjure.us.

Love Drawing & Self Love

This soap is perfect for supporting love drawing workings by first addressing our relationship with ourselves. When this soap is used on a daily basis, its ingredients can improve self esteem and increase a positive self image. Remember: we become more attractive when we project the confidence that comes from self love.

Fast Luck

When working towards matters of finances or money use our Fast Luck Soap everyday. This soap contains a recipe specially created for attracting increased income. Use this soap in conjunction with other spiritual money workings to increase its effects.

Uncrossing

Use this soap in between spiritual baths to maintain the beneficial effects of the bath. When contending with difficult circumstances that weigh on us, we can use Uncrossing Soap everyday to counteract mild depression, misplaced anger, confusion, or any and all emotional distress.

Coffee Cleanse

Coffee is a classic cleansing agent in hoodoo practice. Our Coffee Cleanse Soap has a similar effect as our Uncrossing Soap—use when even just a small boost is needed to make it through the day.

CURIOS

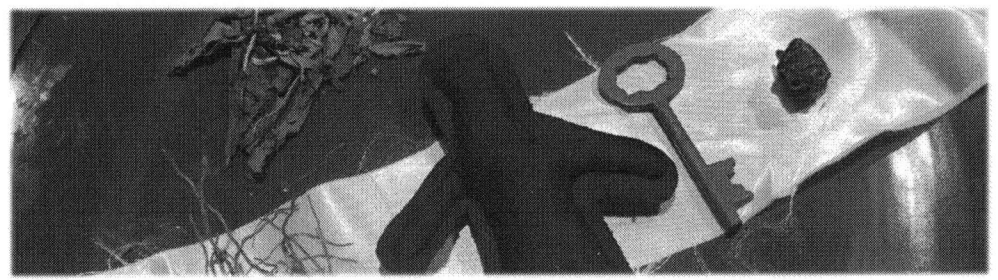

WHAT ARE HOODOO CURIOS AND HOW ARE THEY USED?

The word "curio" is an umbrella terms for any magical tool that doesn't fit into one of the more common categories. Curios can range from multi-layered charms and talismans to simple items that are meant to be carried or worn. These items have been fashioned by a conjure man to work in ways that are tailored to a specific client's needs.

The creation of a curio relies on the knowledge and expertise of the person who creates it so that it can be used at its most effective. Multi-layered curio items combine several hoodoo techniques and they operate in multi-faceted ways to produce the strongest results. Examples of simple curios include roots, sticks, stones, bones, keys, and countless other items that have been blessed and treated with empowering rituals.

Curios are made with both traditional and new recipes that can be crafted by a hoodoo practitioner. Curios usually come with instructions that are unique to the particular item.

As noted earlier, curios are created with a specific intent. In order to best learn how to work with your personal curio, it is very important to have a conversation with whomever created it.

Curios
Our Products

For more detailed descriptions of our curios, visit us online at www.crescentcityconjure.us.

Blessed Railroad Spikes

Our railroad spikes are used to protect the home. Nail one spike into each of the four cardinal directions (or the four corners) of the house. For use in offices or if living in a rented apartment or home, stand the spikes up vertically in the four cardinal direction of the space. Be sure to feed the spikes by refreshing them with protection oil and small amounts of rum.

Coffin Nail Cross

A small charm for protection. Hang this charm above doorways and windows in the home or places of work. May also be hung from the rearview mirror of a vehicle or from key chains.

Protection Chicken's Foot Charm

This charm is especially good at protection against negative spiritual work and witchcraft. Use this charm by hanging it above doorways and windows or in the car.

Gambler's Luck Charm

Carry this charm in the left pocket when playing games of chance; it will protect against costly financial losses while also assisting in the drawing luck.

Curios

Authentic Four Thieves Vinegar

France, c. 1600:

The lore of the Four Thieves Vinegar...

The black plague raged. The town of Toulouse was beset with robbers. Perfumers by day, four of these most infamous criminals operated under the veil of night. Without a hint of fear, these bold thieves walked among the dead and dying, plundering homes and business as the dreaded plague claimed the night's victims.

Eventually caught, a judge offered a deal in exchange for their lives: were they to reveal the secret of their continued health and resistance to the plague, then they would be given a full pardon from their crimes.

Their secret? A vinegar based herb preparation. The Four Thieves doused themselves from head to toe before entering their victims' homes. The herbs used in their formula contained strong antibacterial agents, as well as essential oils that had the power to repel insects. When these herbs were added to apple cider vinegar they were proved to create a potent disinfectant.

Use our Authentic Four Thieves Vinegar to prevent illness. Dilute a small cap of this vinegar in an 8oz. glass of water and drink at the onset of colds or flus. You may also add a small amount to spiritual baths and washes for added healing.

OTHER PRODUCTS

INKS

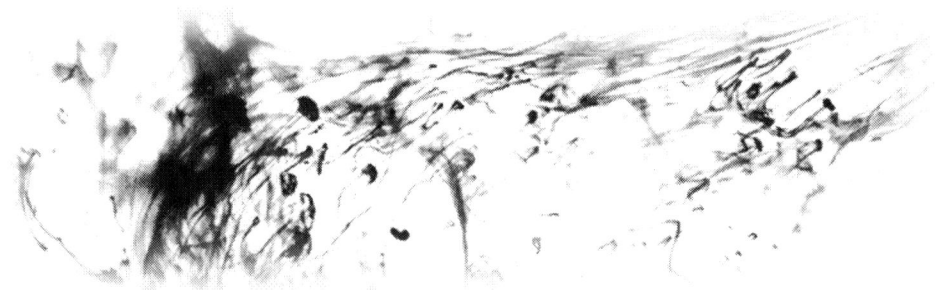

For more information, please visit us at www.crescentcityconjure.us.

DRAGON'S BLOOD & DOVE'S BLOOD

Use magical inks with fountain or calligraphy pens to add power to written spells. Use Dragon's Blood in spells for protection, sexuality, and empowerment. Use Dove's Blood in spells for love and romance.

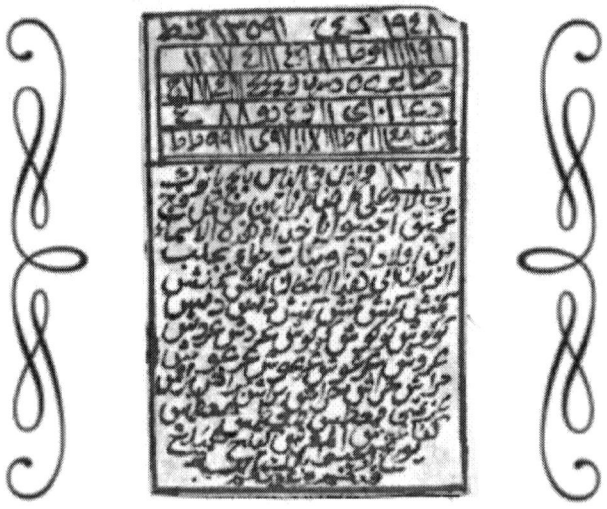

Other Products
Spiritual Incense

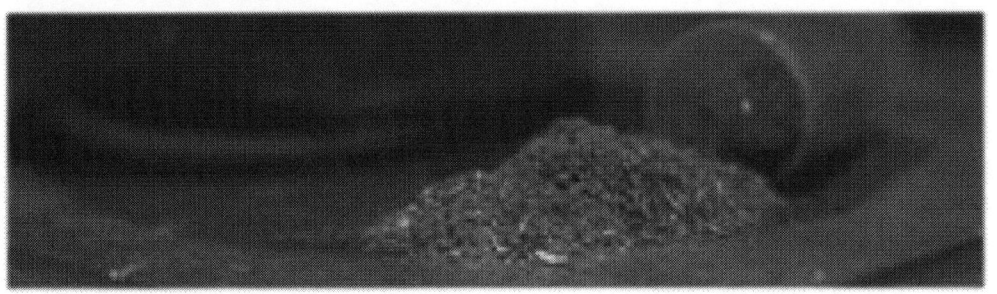

What are spiritual incense and how are they used?

Spiritual incense are used during prayers and spell work to amplify the results and send blessings upward to God. Walk through the smoke of the incense to carry the blessing with you throughout your day. Bless talismans, charms, and curios by passing them through the smoke. All of our incense at Crescent City Conjure are hand-blended recipes of herbs and resins which release a pleasant smell when burned.

For more information, please visit us at www.crescentcityconjure.us.

Prosperity Drawing Incense

Use on charcoal to burn and release blessings of money drawing and increased income. Place a small amount on a hot charcoal in your home or business. You may also use the incense as a powder to sprinkle where prosperity is needed.

Closing Words

These directions are intended to provide the information that you need in order to use our spiritual tools with confidence. If you are new to your spiritual practice, please do not become discouraged as you learn and grow in your proficiency.

This practice may seem simple on the surface, but the small details and intricacies make it extremely specified. Every ingredient, every recipe, every knot, and every word, should be carefully considered in the working of every spell.

If your workings have not manifested in the space of a month or so, then it is okay to try again. Identify what may have gone wrong and work to correct any mistakes in a second attempt. The results of your work will take time to develop and they may not be apparent right away. Be patient!

As a spiritual practitioner of twenty-plus years, I have witnessed the manifestation of countless spells; not only for my clients, but for myself as well. I have observed the energy that is called upon in magical workings. It is undeniably powerful. That power unfolds in very specific ways, providing me insight into what's to come. As an experienced conjure man, the variables that effect the outcomes of workings have become predictable to me. These are the things that I take into account before performing any working.

Crescent City Conjure will soon release "Hoodoo Instructions," an even more comprehensive book that will comprise my own personal experiences of the past two decades. It will include in depth descriptions and secrets of powerful spell work.

Blessings,

From Sen Elias
and the Crescent City Conjure Family

Manufactured by Amazon.ca
Bolton, ON